INVENTIONS THAT CHANGED THE WORLD

ROBERT GODDARD and the ROCKET

I0808406

Louise Spilsbury

PowerKiDS press
NEW YORK

Published in 2016 by **The Rosen Publishing Group**
29 East 21st Street, New York, NY 10010

Copyright © 2016 by The Rosen Publishing Group

All rights reserved. No part of this book may be reproduced in any form without permission in writing from the publisher, except by a reviewer.

Produced for Rosen by Calcium

Editors for Calcium: Harriet McGregor and Sarah Eason
Designers: Jessica Moon and Paul Myerscough
Picture Research: Harriet McGregor

Picture credits: Cover: Getty Images: ullstein bild (fg); Getty Images: Hulton Archive (bkgd). Insides: Library of Congress: Detroit Publishing Company 6; NASA: 4, 9, 10, 13, 14, 16, 17, 19, 22, 23, 25, 26–27, 27, 28, 19, GSFC 5, National Geographic Society 18–19; Shutterstock: Everett Historical 21, Suppakij1017 11; Wikimedia Commons: 7, Al Blasko 15, Lisa Shea 12.

Cataloging-in-Publication Data

Spilsbury, Louise.
Robert Goddard and the rocket / by Louise Spilsbury.
p. cm. — (Inventions that changed the world)
Includes index.
ISBN 978-1-5081-4639-1 (pbk.)
ISBN 978-1-5081-4640-7 (6-pack)
ISBN 978-1-5081-4641-4 (library binding)
1. Goddard, Robert Hutchings, — 1882-1945 — Juvenile literature.
2. Rocketry — United States — Biography — Juvenile literature.
I. Spilsbury, Louise. II. Title.
TL781.85.G6 S65 2016
621.43'56—d23

Manufactured in the United States of America

CPSIA Compliance Information: Batch #BW16PK: For Further Information contact Rosen Publishing, New York, New York at 1-800-237-9932

CONTENTS

BLAST OFF!

When Robert Goddard invented his now-famous rocket in 1926, he changed the world. It took years for his invention to receive the attention it truly deserved, but today Robert Goddard is recognized as the man who unlocked the secret of rockets and space travel.

EARLY ROCKETS

The first rockets may have been discovered by accident. By around the year 1000, the Chinese had invented **gunpowder**. To make exciting explosions for festivals, they filled bamboo tubes with gunpowder and threw them into a fire. It is thought that when one of these tubes failed to explode, the gases produced by the burning gunpowder shot it out of the fire instead. Once they learned that gunpowder tubes could launch themselves with the power of the escaping gas, the Chinese attached rockets to arrows to shoot fire at their enemies over long distances.

ROCKETS, THEN AND NOW

Over the next 700 years, many people experimented with rockets, all the time improving the type of gunpowder used to increase the distance rockets could travel.

Buzz Aldrin's famous walk on the moon in 1969 was only possible because of rocket technology.

People continued to use solid-fuel powered rockets to shoot fire arrows in wars. However, their aim was inaccurate, so after the invention of more precise **artillery** weapons, such as cannons, armies no longer used rockets. It was not until the end of the nineteenth century and into the early twentieth century that people started to develop ideas about rockets that would lead to a new, controllable version that would one day enter space.

From early in his childhood, Robert Goddard was fascinated by how rockets worked and how far they could reach into the sky.

The Word Is...

Even at high school, Robert had big ideas. As part of his oration at his class's graduation, he famously said:

"It has often proved true that the dream of yesterday is the hope of today, and the reality of tomorrow."

EARLY IDEAS

Robert Hutchings Goddard was born in Worcester, Massachusetts, on October 5, 1882. His father, Nahum Danford Goddard, was a bookkeeper who worked for a machine store that made knives for paper and textile factories. His mother was Fannie Louise Hoyt, daughter of the owner of the machine store where Nahum worked.

INTEREST IN INVENTION

When Robert was young, Worcester was a busy, energetic city full of factories and workshops that made a variety of things, from razors and shoes to machine tools and plows. Products made in Worcester were sold all over the world. Surrounded by industry, it is perhaps no surprise that young Robert became fascinated by physics, mechanics, and how things worked. Unfortunately, Robert was often sick as a child and was absent from school for long periods of time. He read a lot during this time and learned to share his father's interest in technology and inventions. He may have been intrigued by Nahum's invention of a machine knife for cutting rabbit hair!

DREAMING OF SPACE

In 1898, Robert read H.G. Wells' sci-fi novel *The War of the Worlds*, about Martians invading planet Earth, which was being serialized in the *Boston Post* newspaper.

H. G. Wells' novel *The War of the Worlds* inspired Robert. This image is taken from the novel, published in 1898, and shows aliens attempting to make their home on Earth.

The idea of space fascinated Robert. On October 19, 1899, after climbing into an old cherry tree to cut away its dead branches, he instead began daydreaming about building a machine that could fly into space. He said later that this moment changed his life forever, and every year after this he made October 19 his "Anniversary Day," when he took a day's vacation to concentrate on his project.

At the turn of the twentieth century, Worcester, Massachusetts, was a center of machinery and manufacturing. Union Station, shown here in 1906, was built in 1875.

The Word Is...

Robert wrote in his autobiography about his moment of inspiration in the cherry tree:

"It was one of the quiet, colorful afternoons of sheer beauty which we have in October in New England, and as I looked toward the fields at the east, I imagined how wonderful it would be to make some device which had even the possibility of ascending to Mars, and how it would look on a small scale, if sent up from the meadow at my feet."

AT COLLEGE

Although Robert had missed out on schooling when he was a young boy, he proved to be an excellent student later. His sharp mind was also matched by a burning desire to invent.

A STUDENT OF DISTINCTION

Robert graduated from South High School, Worcester, in 1904. He then began studying at Worcester Polytechnic Institute, where his enthusiasm for experimenting with rockets almost got him expelled. In 1908, he attempted to fire a rocket from the basement of the physics building, creating a huge cloud of smoke! Luckily, school officials realized Robert was a promising student who had not meant to cause trouble, and allowed him to finish his studies. Robert's exam results were described as spectacular, and he went on to earn both a master's and doctorate degree in physics from Clark University. After he got his doctorate in 1911, Robert immediately began teaching physics at the same university.

ROCKET ENGINE RESEARCH

Robert began experiments with rockets in earnest at Clark University. He launched his first gunpowder rocket in 1915. When he realized that only 2 percent of the energy available from a gunpowder rocket was used to make the rocket move, he began to work on other ways to improve the parts that made up the rocket. He replaced the nozzle on his rocket with a new design that increased his rocket's efficiency. In 1916, he carried out experiments to prove that a rocket could work in a vacuum because it does not need air to push against. This was an important discovery for the man who wanted to send rockets into the vacuum of space!

Successful Partners

It was while he was working at Clark University that Robert met his wife, Esther Christine Kisk, who worked as a secretary to Clark University's president. Esther left the university after she married Robert, to help him with his work. She was an enthusiastic supporter and by filming and photographing his rocket experiments, Esther proved to be very important in recording Robert's research.

Robert with the vacuum tube device he built in 1916, to prove that rockets did not need air to push against in order to move in space.

EXPLOSIVE EXPERIMENTS

By 1916, Robert was carrying out flight tests using gunpowder-propelled rockets near Worcester. When some of these rockets exploded, they shot up to 500 feet (150 m) into the air.

TESTING GROUNDS

In order to continue his work, Robert needed funding, and in 1917, he was awarded a $5,000 grant from the Smithsonian Institution in Washington, D.C. His research was put on hold, however, when the United States entered World War I (1914–1918) that year, and Robert began working for the US Army designing rockets and launchers for use in battle. In November 1918, Robert successfully demonstrated several rockets at the Aberdeen Proving Ground in Maryland. Powered by solid fuel, the rockets were launched from a long tube and could have been used to deliver bombs over a distance of 1 mile (1.6 km), but the war ended shortly after his display.

Robert made small model rockets to carry out experiments that could help him launch and fly full-sized rockets.

RESEARCH AND RIDICULE

Robert returned to Clark University and carried on his rocket research. In 1920, he wrote a report about how he was using the Smithsonian funding. It was called "*A Method of Reaching Extreme Altitude*." In it, he described using rockets to send weather-recording instruments into the **atmosphere**, as well as other research. Near the end, he mentioned the possibility of a rocket reaching the moon. When *The New York Times* reporters saw the work, they and reporters of other newspapers ridiculed Robert and his ideas, calling him "Moon Man." They even suggested he lacked the knowledge of students studying basic physics. The insults hurt, but they did not stop Robert. Instead, he returned to the idea he had first developed in 1914, for a liquid-fueled rocket. By 1924, he had developed a working design and knew he was close to a breakthrough.

The *Boston Herald* also mocked Robert's work. Its headline read: "New Rocket Devised By Prof. Goddard May Hit Face of The Moon."

Other Inventors

While Robert was designing his rockets, he was unaware that inventors in other countries were heading toward similar discoveries. In Russia, a schoolteacher named Konstantin Tsiolkovsky, and in Germany, Hermann Oberth, both published papers about rocket science around the same time. The three scientists did not know that they were all working on such similar research and all three are considered to be important figures in the history of rocket development.

THE FAMOUS ROCKET

Robert spent the next couple of years working on his rocket design whenever he could. By early 1926, he had successfully lifted a liquid-fueled rocket within a fixed stand for about 12 seconds inside his lab, and was ready to take the tests outside.

This monument marks the spot of Robert's famous first rocket launch.

MAKING HISTORY

On March 16, 1926, in Auburn, Massachusetts, Robert launched a 10-foot (3 m) rocket from a 7-foot (2 m) frame. He nicknamed the rocket *Nell* and set it off from a farm in Auburn, about 2 miles (3 km) away from the university. *Nell* was powered by a combination of liquid oxygen and gasoline, but when this fuel mix was first lit, nothing happened. It burned for about 20 seconds, then the fuel tank suddenly ignited and *Nell* shot into the air, flying at about 60 miles (96 km) per hour! In just 2.5 seconds, the rocket had climbed 41 feet (14 m) before crashing into the ground.

The rocket flew a distance of 184 feet (56 m) from the launching frame. This was a historic moment: *Nell* was the first-ever rocket to be launched using liquid fuel. Unfortunately, although Esther was recording the experiment, the camera ran out of film while the fuel tank was lighting and there is no photographic record of this first historic flight.

The Word Is...

Robert described the first flight of his liquid-fueled rocket in his diary:

"Even though the release was pulled, the rocket did not rise at first, but the flame came out, and there was a steady roar. After a number of seconds, it rose, slowly until it cleared the frame, and then at express train speed, curving over to the left, and striking the ice and snow, still going at a rapid rate. It looked almost magical as it rose, without any appreciably greater noise or flame, as if it said 'I've been here long enough; I think I'll be going somewhere else, if you don't mind.'"

Robert with his liquid oxygen-gasoline rocket in its launch frame at Auburn.

HOW IT WORKED

The first successful flight of that liquid-fueled rocket was the moment Robert had been working toward for many years, since the day in the cherry tree when he first dreamed of space flight. Here was a rocket design that could one day be scaled up to make flights into space. But how exactly might that work?

ROCKET SCIENCE

When the gunpowder in a firework is set alight, the burning powder makes hot gases that shoot downward out of a hole, pushing the firework upward. Robert's rocket worked in a similar way, but it burned gasoline and liquid oxygen to achieve liftoff. When this fuel is burned inside an enclosed space called a **combustion chamber**, a **chemical reaction** takes place, creating very hot, expanding gases. At the end of the combustion chamber is a hole that leads to the nozzle. The hot gases shoot out of the nozzle, into the air below. As the gases are pushed out of the end of the upright rocket, they create **thrust**, which pushes the rocket upward into the air.

Robert spent more than two years working on a system for pumping the liquid oxygen and the gasoline into the engine of his rocket.

TACKLING PROBLEMS

Robert's rocket had two pipes into the combustion chamber, one carrying gasoline and the other carrying liquid oxygen. Burning oxygen requires very high temperatures that could have damaged the combustion chamber. Robert solved this by having the liquid oxygen, on its way from the fuel tank, cool the combustion chamber. Another problem Robert faced was controlling the rocket in flight. He tried to make the flight more stable by mounting the rocket above the fuel tank, with the tank shielded from the flame by a metal cone. Although the design worked, it was not as stable as he had hoped.

Thrust and Gravity

Forces always work in pairs. This is called action and reaction. When a rocket is on the ground, the force of **gravity** pulling it downward is stronger than thrust forces pushing upward, so it stays still. When the thrust forces (created by gases from burning rocket fuel) pushing a rocket upward are stronger than the gravity forces pulling it downward, the rocket will lift off. This is an example of one of Sir Isaac Newton's fundamental laws: "For every action, there is an equal and opposite reaction."

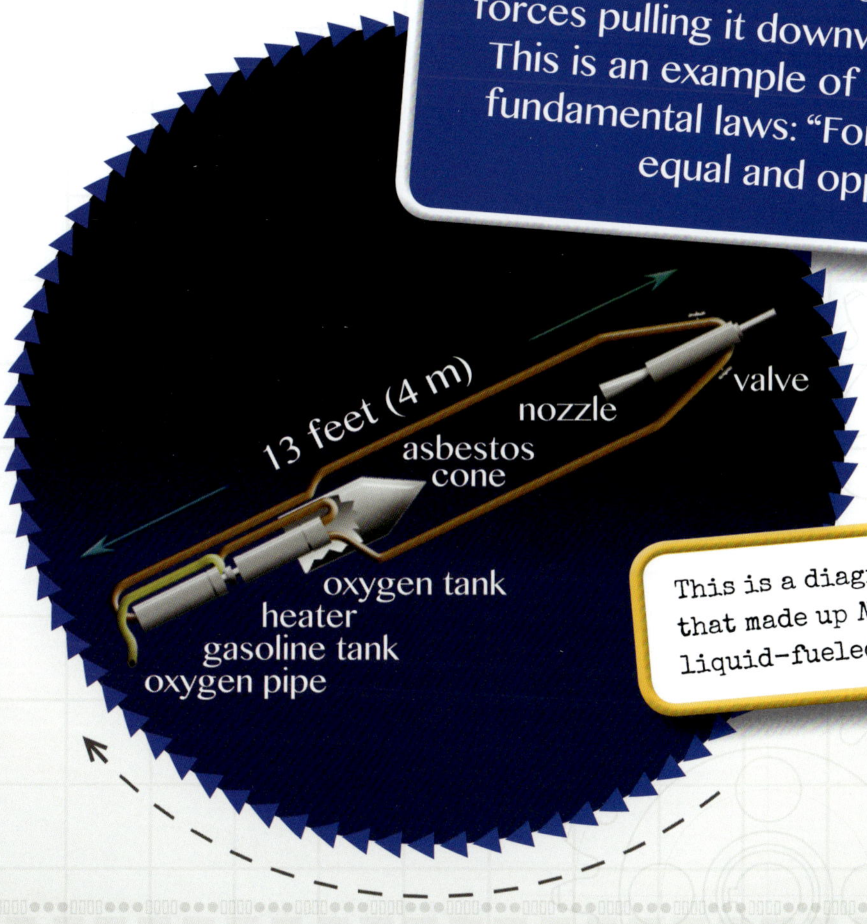

This is a diagram showing the parts that made up *Nell*, Robert's first liquid-fueled rocket.

ROCKET DEVELOPER

Following the historic flight of his first successful rocket, Robert decided that he needed to build bigger rockets to be able to carry out further tests. He also began work on developing a bigger, better launch tower from which to fire his rockets into the air.

THE 1929 ROCKET

Robert's new rockets could carry much more fuel than his first rocket and used an electrically fired igniter instead of the gunpowder-fired igniter. However, his first attempts failed and the rockets tipped over after they were ignited. Robert did not give up. Whenever he failed, he simply started again. In July 17, 1929, Robert launched his most elaborate rocket so far. It was equipped with a barometer, thermometer, and a camera so that it could take readings during its flight. The rocket reached 90 feet (27 m) into the air during an 18.5-second flight and flew a distance of 171 feet (52 m). The science equipment on board was ejected safely via parachute, and recovered later.

MAKING HEADLINES

The 1929 rocket launches made headlines and attracted the attention of Charles Lindbergh, the first man to fly alone across the Atlantic Ocean. Charles was interested in how rockets might be used in aircraft, and he first visited Robert on November 23, 1929. He believed that the rocket was an important invention that could change the world. He introduced Robert to Harvey Guggenheim, a millionaire who provided Robert with a large amount of money to help him continue his research. Another important development was that in 1930, Clark University granted Robert leave from his teaching duties so that he could concentrate all his time and attention on his rocket designs.

The Word Is...

When the 1929 rocket crashed back down to the ground, it exploded noisily and set fire to a field. It was so noisy and bright that people thought an airplane had crashed. Robert described the scene:

"Owing to the flight being the highest so far attained, and the flame using an excess of gasoline producing a loud noise and a bright white flare, neighbors sent in calls for ambulances, thinking that an airplane had caught fire and crashed. Unknown to me, two police ambulances searched through Auburn for "victims," and an airplane was sent from the Grafton airport for the same purpose . . ."

The 1929 crash scared local people, so Robert moved his launch area to Camp Devens, an artillery range 25 miles (40 km) from Worcester. He made 16 fixed-engine test firings, but didn't launch rockets there.

TESTING, TESTING

In July 1930, Robert moved his laboratory to Roswell, New Mexico. From then on, Robert was free to work full-time on building and testing rockets.

WORKING IN PEACE

There were likely several reasons for the move to Roswell. The area was remote, with no buildings for miles. It was therefore the perfect place for Robert to work on rockets in safety and without the risk of disturbing any neighbors, as he had done at the Auburn site. He also needed a site with plenty of level ground, high up with good visibility all around, and which was not too windy, wet, or cloudy. At Roswell, Robert could also work in secrecy, a need which may have been partly due to the potential military use of his invention. Working in a remote area also kept Robert away from the newspaper reporters whom he had grown to distrust and dislike. Working in private would help Robert to avoid negative publicity.

ROCKETS IN ROSWELL

Robert launched his first rocket in Roswell on December 30, 1930. It had a new gas pressure tank to force the liquid oxygen and gasoline into the combustion chamber. It reached a height of 2,000 feet (610 m) and a speed of 500 miles per hour (800 kph). Over the following 15 years, Robert launched 48 rockets, of which 31 achieved liftoff. He made more improvements to his rocket design, including adding **vanes** linked to a **gyroscope** within the rocket's nose, in order to stabilize the rocket in flight. However, the highest rocket he ever launched was the *L-13*, which only reached a height of 1.7 miles (2.7 km) in 22.3 seconds on March 26, 1937.

Robert (left) building a rocket at his workshop in Roswell with Nils Ljungquist, Albert Kisk, and Charles Mansur.

Robert and his team carrying a rocket that had been damaged during a test flight back to the workshop.

Dogged Determination

Robert faced more challenges. In 1932, the Guggenheim grant was suddenly canceled because of the financial difficulties caused by the **Great Depression**. Robert went back to work at Clark University, but luckily a grant from the Smithsonian Institution allowed him to continue laboratory testing. Another grant from a new Guggenheim foundation allowed him to continue testing rockets at Roswell from September 1934.

WORLD WAR II

During World War II (1939-1945), Robert met with army officers to discuss ways of using what he had learned about liquid-fueled rockets to help the military improve their aircraft.

JATO

Robert closed down the Roswell laboratory and started to work from a lab at the Naval Engineering Experiment Station at Annapolis, in Maryland. There he worked on ways to provide rocket assisted takeoff for heavy bombers and other aircraft. This became known as "Jet-Assisted Takeoff," or "JATO." During this period, Robert also supervised the development of a liquid-fueled JATO unit for flying boats, so that they could land and take off from the ocean. He continued working at the military laboratory until 1945.

V-2 ROCKET

Although the US military was not interested in Robert's rocket designs, the German military was. German rocket developers studied Robert's **patent** applications and ideas, and used them as the starting point to build their own rockets. By 1944, the Germans had developed the famous V-2, a liquid-fueled rocket that shot up to 50 miles (80 km) high in the air before hurtling toward its target on the ground, where its warhead exploded. The V-2 was stable in the air, could travel long distances, and could be aimed at a target, so it caused many deaths.

ROBERT AND THE BAZOOKA

Although none of the rocket designs Robert worked on for the military in World War I had entered service, a small, handheld rocket launcher known as a bazooka was developed in World War II, as a weapon for use against tanks. Variants of the bazooka are now called "rocket-propelled grenades," or RPGs. The design was based on ideas Robert developed and demonstrated in 1918, at the Aberdeen Proving Ground in Maryland.

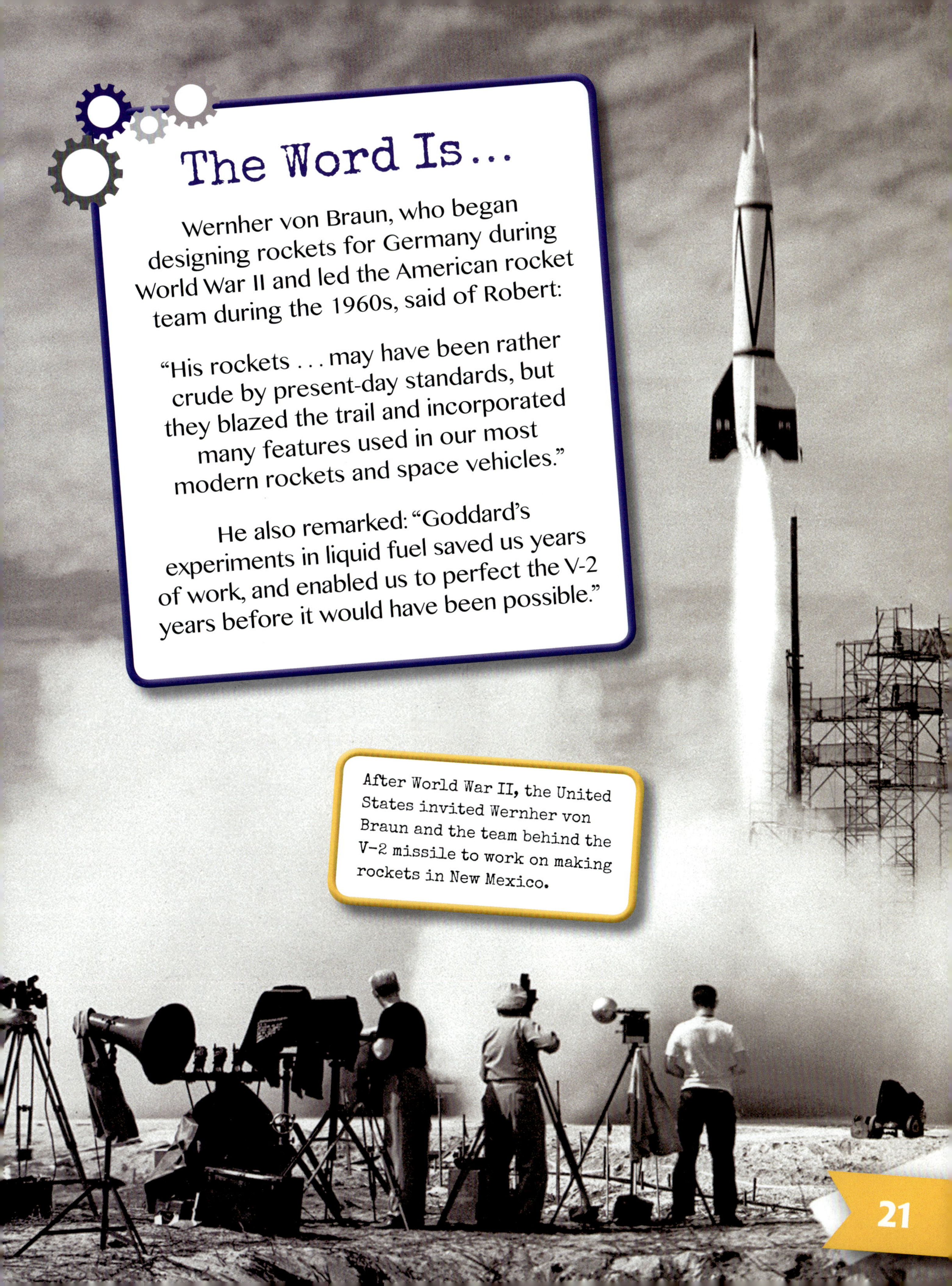

The Word Is...

Wernher von Braun, who began designing rockets for Germany during World War II and led the American rocket team during the 1960s, said of Robert:

"His rockets . . . may have been rather crude by present-day standards, but they blazed the trail and incorporated many features used in our most modern rockets and space vehicles."

He also remarked: "Goddard's experiments in liquid fuel saved us years of work, and enabled us to perfect the V-2 years before it would have been possible."

After World War II, the United States invited Wernher von Braun and the team behind the V-2 missile to work on making rockets in New Mexico.

END OF DAYS

Robert had never been a completely healthy man, and after moving to Maryland, his health grew worse. In 1945, his doctors broke the bad news to Robert that he had throat cancer. He continued to work, even though he could barely speak and could only whisper, until his condition worsened, resulting in surgery. Robert died not long afterward, in August 1945, at his home in Baltimore, Maryland.

ESTHER'S ENDEAVORS

In spite of all his hard work and achievements, Robert's work on rocket science remained largely overlooked at the time of his death. After his funeral took place in Hope Cemetery in his home town of Worcester, Massachusetts, Esther worked tirelessly to publicize his work and publish some more of his writings. She also applied for patents for inventions she knew should be credited to Robert. Her hard work paid off and Robert was credited with 214 patents, of which 131 were filed by Esther after his death. In 1960, the government agreed to pay Esther and the Guggenheim Foundation $1 million for using information in Robert's patents in US missile and rocket programs.

On March 16, 1961, the new NASA research center was named in honor of the United States' great rocket innovator, Robert Goddard.

FAME AFTER DEATH

Robert was not famous during his lifetime. Later, as people began to acknowledge his contribution to science, he was awarded many honors. On September 16, 1959, the US Congress ordered a special gold medal to be made in his honor and the American Rocket Society, the American Institute of Aeronautics and Astronautics, and other organizations created Goddard awards and fellowships. The Goddard Memorial Library at Clark University was named in his honor. One of the greatest tributes was naming NASA's Space Flight Center in Greenbelt, Maryland, after Robert. Esther attended the dedication of NASA's Goddard Space Flight Center on March 16, 1961, 35 years to the day that Robert launched the first liquid-fueled rocket from his aunt's farm.

The Goddard Space Flight Center was designed to test rockets and other equipment in facilities that simulate the space environment.

The Word Is...

Although Robert must have been disappointed not to see his dream of a rocket traveling into space during his lifetime, it is likely he still believed that it was only a matter of time before it happened. He himself said:

"Just remember, when you think all is lost, the future remains."

THE SPACE RACE

After World War II, the German scientists who had developed the V-2 rocket based on Robert's discoveries in the 1930s helped the United States and the Soviet Union design spacecraft. Between 1955 and 1972, the United States and the Soviet Union competed to become the first to reach and control space. The space race had begun.

THE RACE INTO SPACE

The Russians were the first to take the lead in the space race when they launched *Sputnik I*, the first successful **satellite**, into orbit on October 4, 1957. US satellite *Explorer I* was launched four months later. Then on April 12, 1961, the Russians had another triumph when Yuri Gagarin became the first man to orbit Earth, on *Vostok I*. Astronaut John Glenn became the first American to orbit Earth on February 20, 1962, on the *Friendship 7* spacecraft. This made the Americans determined to be the first to put a man on the moon, and on July 20, 1969, Neil Armstrong and Edwin Aldrin stepped out of their *Apollo 11* spacecraft onto the moon. By 1975, relations between the United States and the Soviet Union had improved and they took part in a joint space mission, the *Apollo-Soyez* project.

Yuri and Robert

When Yuri became the first man in space, he had Robert to thank. It was Robert who had come up with the idea that a spacecraft could go faster and higher if it were propelled into space by a large rocket and one or more small rockets. The large rocket provided the spacecraft with thrust power to escape Earth's gravity, then dropped off. Without this extra weight, the spacecraft could speed up and continue its journey, leaving behind other extra smaller rockets if necessary along the way. The multistage rocket was one of the most important inventions of space exploration.

The multistage rocket system made possible the launch of space vehicles such as *Apollo 14*, shown here at the Kennedy Space Center in 1970.

ROBERT'S LEGACY

Robert's hard work and creative genius earned him little credit in the United States until the development of spacecraft. When American rocket scientists began to build rockets and launch satellites they realized that it was impossible to do so without acknowledging Robert's work.

ROBERT'S DISCOVERIES

Robert's research gave us many of our basic ideas about rocket propulsion. Most rockets that deliver spacecraft and satellites into Earth's orbit, or travel between planets, use a liquid fuel system, just as Robert's did. He proved that rockets could provide thrust in a vacuum and could work beyond Earth's atmosphere. He figured out a calculation for the speed a rocket must reach in order to escape Earth's gravitational pull. He came up with the idea of gyroscopes to stabilize rockets and vanes to help them steer. He also developed the method of using a rocket's liquid fuel to cool the engine and keep it from melting.

Apollo 11, a multistage rocket, launches from Earth on its mission to the moon, with Neil Armstrong and Edwin Aldrin on board.

Many of the features in Robert's rockets are still used in today's rockets. They were used to build the International Space Station (ISS) and perhaps, one day, will help take humans to Mars.

This image of Earth, as seen from just above the surface of the moon, was taken from *Apollo 11*.

A PUBLIC APOLOGY

Robert did not live to see space rockets take flight or to see the copy of *The New York Times* newspaper printed the day after *Apollo 11* took off for the moon, in July 1969. The paper wrote a correction to its 1920 article, which had mocked him. The newspaper also made a public apology to Robert. At last, the man whose liquid-fuel rocket changed the world had the credit he rightly deserved.

The Word Is...

William Townsend, a Deputy Director of the NASA Goddard Space Flight Center, acknowledged that Robert's first rocket flight contributed directly to space flight becoming a reality. He said:

"That flight became the underpinning of everything that we are able to do in space today and which we take for granted."

TIMELINE

1882 On October 5, Robert Hutchings Goddard is born in Worcester, Massachusetts.

1899 On October 19, Robert has a daydream about building a machine that can fly into space.

1915 Robert launches his first gunpowder rocket.

In 1916, Robert built this vacuum tube device and experimented with ways to improve rocket efficiency.

1924 On June 21, Robert marries Esther Christine Kisk.

1926 On March 16, Robert launches the world's first successful liquid-fueled rocket.

1942 The German V-2 is the first rocket to reach 62 miles (100 km) from Earth's surface, the boundary of space.

1957 On October 4, Russia's *Sputnik I* becomes the first successful satellite in orbit.

1957 Russian space dog Laika becomes the first animal to orbit Earth on *Sputnik 2*.

1958 US satellite *Explorer I* is launched and, as well as orbiting Earth, it gathers useful scientific data.

1959 Russian spacecraft *Luna 1* becomes the first to fly beyond Earth's orbit and the first to orbit the sun.

1961 NASA's Space Flight Center in Maryland is named after Goddard.

1961 On April 12, cosmonaut Yuri Gagarin becomes the first man to orbit Earth in space on the Russian spacecraft *Vostok I*.

1962 On February 20, astronaut John Glenn becomes the first American to orbit Earth in space.

1965 Cosmonaut Alexei Leonov carries out the first-ever spacewalk from the *Voskhod* spacecraft.

1969 On July 20, astronaut Neil Armstrong becomes the first person to walk on the moon when he steps out of the US *Apollo 11* spacecraft.

1969 An unmanned US spacecraft, *Mariner 6*, makes a close flyby of Mars.

1971 In July, Russia's *Salyut 1*, the world's first space station, is launched from an unmanned rocket.

1973 The United States launches *Skylab*, a space station that remains in orbit for six years.

1975 The United States and the Soviet Union take part in a joint space mission. Astronauts and cosmonauts dock the last Apollo spacecraft with the Soviet vessel *Soyuz*, and the crews visit each other's crafts.

1976 On July 20, the first of two *Viking* probes touches down on the surface of Mars.

1977 United States' *Voyager 1* and *2* deep space probes launch.

1978 The *Pioneer Venus* probe becomes the first US probe to enter the atmosphere of the planet Venus.

1981 The first flight of the manned, reusable space shuttle *Columbia* takes place.

1984 Sally Ride becomes the first US woman in space.

Robert Goddard in Auburn, ready to test his rocket designs. The rocket is set in the tower behind Robert and his co-workers.

1995 The unmanned *Galileo* spacecraft arrives at Jupiter to carry out an eight-year mission of exploration.

1997 US rover the *Sojourner* explores the surface geology on Mars.

1998 The International Space Station (ISS) is established.

2004 Pilot Mike Melville flies *SpaceShipOne* (SS1), the first successful privately manned spacecraft.

2011 US *Messenger* spacecraft begins its year-long mission to orbit and study the planet Mercury.

2012 NASA's *Voyager 1* probe, launched in 1977, enters interstellar space.

2014 *SpaceShipTwo* (SS2), a space plane designed for space tourism, crashes during a test flight.

GLOSSARY

artillery Large guns and weapons used in war.

atmosphere The layer of gases that surrounds a planet and is held in place by gravity.

chemical reaction A process that changes one set of chemical substances into another.

combustion chamber A compartment in an engine where a mix of fuel and air is burned to make the engine work.

forces Pushes or pulls. Forces give energy to an object.

gravity Force of attraction between two objects. Gravity increases with mass, so on Earth, gravity pulls everything toward the ground.

Great Depression A worldwide economic crisis that happened in the 1930s.

gunpowder A black powder made of a mix of chemicals that can explode.

gyroscope A device that has a wheel mounted in such a way that it can turn freely and keep the same direction to help machines maintain balance or direction.

patent A document issued to someone who invents something new, so that other people cannot copy it without permission.

satellite An electronic device placed in orbit around Earth. Weather satellites are used to collect weather information and communications satellites pass on television and radio signals.

thrust A force that moves an object forward or upward.

vanes Wide flat parts such as blades that are fixed to the side of a machine and can push or be pushed by the wind (or water) to help that machine move.

FOR MORE INFORMATION

Books

Chastain, Zachary. *Rocket Technology* (Kid's Library of Space Exploration). New York, NY: Village Earth Press, 2014.

Koll, Hilary, and Steve Mills. *Launch a Rocket into Space* (You Do the Math). Irvine, CA: QEB Publishing, 2015.

Lock, Deborah. *Rocket Science (*DK Readers L3). New York, NY: DK Children, 2015.

Murphy, Maggie. *High-Tech DIY Projects with Flying Objects* (Maker Kids). New York, NY: PowerKids Press, 2014.

Murphy, Pat. *Air Power: Rocket Science Made Simple* (Klutz). New York, NY: Klutz (Scholastic), 2014.

Parker, Steve. *Space Pioneers* (Story of Space). North Mankato, MN: Smart Apple Media, 2016.

Websites

Due to the changing nature of Internet links, PowerKids Press has developed an online list of websites related to the subject of this book. This site is updated regularly. Please use this link to access the list: **www.powerkidslinks.com/itctw/goddard**

INDEX